SOMETIMES LIFE!

WRITTEN BY

VERONA PARKS

SOMETIMES LIFE!

ISBN: 13: 978-0-578-35328-9
4 Corners of Atlanta Editing and Publishing
4Corners-llc.com

ACKNOWLEDGEMENTS

I would like to thank first and foremost my Heavenly Father for the gifts that He has given me. For always providing a vision and the provision. I would also like to thank my Husband Antonio Parks for always believing in my creativity, complimenting my craft, and encouraging me to go for it. Your love is more than anything I could ever write about, but I'll try.

SOMETIMES LIFE!

Chapter 1

Having spent the last six years in college, it was finally over. No more papers or exams. This morning's graduation was the best day of Mariah's life. After the last four hours of drinking and celebrating, it was time to pass out in her bed. The plush pillows and satin sheets were calling her name. Knowing that she didn't have to wake up in the morning for, yet another class is what sent her to sleep with a huge smile on her face. Mariah had only been asleep a few hours when a loud bang at the door made her fall from her bed.

Dusting herself off, she made her way to the door. Throwing her robe on, Mariah couldn't help but wonder who could possibly be banging at her door this time of night. "Who is it?" she yelled, crossing the small space from her bedroom to the living room. "Police, open up."

Unlocking only the deadbolt, Mariah pulled the door open only enough to see for sure that this wasn't a prank. "Let me see some ID," she glared out through the small crack. Holding out a detective's badge, the rather large gentleman stated, "Ma'am, my name is Detective Robins. Are you Ms. Mariah C. Adams?" "Why?" "I'm here regarding a missing person complaint." "Unlatching the chain on the door, Mariah became confused because she had just moved to this apartment two weeks before, and not many people knew she lived there.

Not to mention the landlord already told her that the apartment had been vacant for the previous six months. So, who was missing? "Ms. Adams?" Detective Robins calling her name caught her attention again. "I'm sorry, who exactly is missing?" "Well, according to these files, you are."

Feeling more irritated now than before, Mariah tried to keep her voice steady. "Excuse me, how can I be missing when I'm standing right here?" "Well, Ms. Adams, if you have a minute, I would like to come in and discuss it with you." "Sure, come on in. Excuse the mess; I haven't really had time to get everything unpacked yet," gesturing to the piles of boxes blocking the entrance. "Please have a seat officer, can I offer you anything to drink?" Making himself comfortable on the loveseat, "No, thank you, but maybe you can give me some answers." "Okay," having a seat herself, Mariah, still a bit confused, looked at the file in his hands. "Is that about me?" Opening the thin rusty brown folder Detective Robins began.

"Well, Ms. Adams, I received a missing person report on my desk two days ago. A young man with long locs and a horrible attitude claims that you, his fiancée has gone missing. Do you have any idea who this person looking for you is?" Sighing, Mariah rested her head in her hands. "If this brother with an attitude has beautiful hazel eyes, I know exactly who you're talking about. And just for the record, I am his ex-fiancée." "So, do you want to tell me why he is looking for you?" "His name is Fredrick Miles, and he is crazy. I met Fredrick about a year ago at the mall, and he seemed nice enough, but boy was that a trick."

"To make a long story short, we started dating, and I wound up moving in with him. After that, things got bad because he started acting very jealous. At first, I thought it was sweet. After four months, we got engaged, and he really lost his mind. "He started accusing me of sleeping around because I had late study sessions. He even went so far as to follow me to school one day. After one of my classes, I had to stay and talk to my professor about possibly earning some extra points for the final exam. Suddenly Frederick burst through the door and almost took my professor's head off had he not moved out of the way in time. Security had to be called to escort him off school grounds because he became so irate, cursing and just acting like a lunatic. I was so embarrassed. Luckily after a lot of explaining, I was able to finish out the class so I could graduate."

Taking notes, Detective Robins asked, "So, do you think he is a threat?" "Yes, that's why I moved. I tried to act like everything was o.k. after that happened until I could find another place to live as not to cause any suspicion. And as soon as I found this apartment, I signed the lease, picked up my keys, and went back home as usual. That same night after he went to work, I packed my things and quickly moved into this place to make sure that I was gone by the time he got home. Whatever I couldn't grab just got left. I just figured it was best for me to get out before he would really hurt me."

Looking up from his notes, Detective Robins asked, "What do you mean, really hurt you?" "Well, after the confrontation at school, he slapped me when I got home. He said I made him look bad because I should have taken up for him. And that if I ever embarrassed him again, he would really teach me a lesson." Closing his file and standing up, Detective Robins asked one more question. "Now, this is very important. When you left that night, did you leave anything that might give him so much as a hint of where you are?" "No!" Mariah shot back. "Good. Ms. Adams, I'm sorry to have disturbed you. I think I have everything we need to close this case. And don't worry, none of your information will be passed on. I will simply let him know you're not lost and that his best bet would be to move on."

"But just for your safety, keep this address to yourself for a while and make sure you watch your back. I would hate for Frederick to follow you home one day." "Oh yes, sir, that won't be a problem. I just graduated, and I start a new job downtown in two weeks. He doesn't even know where to look for me anymore," Mariah stated with assurance. "Alright, then make sure you keep this deadbolt on." Handing her his card, "And you call me if you need any help." Graciously taking the card, Mariah let Detective Robins out and locked the door tight. She then went back to her bed and passed out again.

The next morning Mariah woke up to the smell of coffee and bacon. A smile spread across her face. There was only one person who made coffee with a hint of nutmeg and vanilla. Her mama Malina. Sure enough, as she made her way into the kitchen, there was her mother, almost into her sixties and didn't look a day over thirty. Malina's Hispanic heritage was clear to see, standing five foot four inches tall with big chocolate-colored eyes. Even her long salt-n-pepper hair did little to take away from her beauty. Her mom was the only other person who knew where she lived and had an extra key to her place.

"Good morning, sleepy head." Mrs. Adams greeted Mariah with a cup of her famous coffee and a huge hug. "How does my graduate want her eggs this morning?" "Morning mom." Mariah giggled at her mother's over-enthusiasm. "You know it doesn't matter, mom, and you really didn't have to do this." Leaning over, Malina placed a hand over her daughter's. "I know, but I won't get to see you as much once you start working downtown." "Oh, mom, don't be silly. We can still have our Wednesday brunch, and I'll still see you at church on Sundays." "O.k. I'm gonna hold you to that. And don't forget that weekend after next, your grandmother is gonna be in town, and we're all going to church. So, don't make any plans for that weekend." "Not a problem, mom. I already set that day aside in my scheduler. And speaking of appointments, don't you have one in about two hours?"

Malina looked down at her watch. "I almost forgot about that," she said with a sneaky look on her face. "Yeah, uh-huh. Thank you for breakfast, but you have got to get going. I don't want to hear anything about you having to reschedule again." Grabbing her mother's coat off the coat rack, Mariah kissed her goodbye. Shaking her head at her mother's antics, once again, she was going to try to find an excuse to not go and get her mammogram done. For a woman her age, especially a black woman with mixed heritage, getting an annual mammogram is vital to your health. If it hadn't been for her aunt's last mammogram, they wouldn't have known about the small cancer tumor growing in her breast.

Thank God they found it in time. After only a short period of chemotherapy, her favorite aunt Janice is now cancer-free.

Looking up at her kitchen, Mariah sighed. Her mom was great at cooking, but cleaning everything up after that was her problem. Breakfast was good, but it would take all of twenty minutes to clean up the mess. Making sure all of the locks were on, Mariah made her way over to the sink to start the clean-up process. Preferring to get it done quickly, less not get it done at all.

Chapter 2

Evan stretched his arms and legs. He had been at his desk for the last six hours straight and was beginning to get writer's block. As a journalist, there was no room for the loss of ideas in his field. Maybe a quick trip down to the coffee shop would help. He did love their Java Chip Frappuccinos with extra whip. They had become a weekly affair he had to have. He could definitely use the caffeine boost the way he was feeling right now.

After letting his supervisor know he was taking a quick break, Evan made his way down the stairs from the eighth floor of his twenty-story office building. He crossed the street to the local coffee shop Clara's café to order his favorite drink and a cranberry walnut muffin. Evan usually took it back with him to work, but he decided to eat there today. Clara's had a few outdoor tables with huge orange umbrellas, so he made himself comfortable at one closest to the fenced-in area.

Taking in a deep breath, he said grace and took a long swig of the chocolaty goodness that sat before him. He always did love the fresh air, which was one of the reasons he moved to Georgia. He figured the air in the south would be much better than what he was used to breathing in New York and Michigan, where he had lived before.

Evan wasn't really one to stay in one place for too long, especially if he didn't see himself getting anywhere. At least anywhere he wanted to get. Hopefully, this would be his last move. Things were going well at work; now, he just wanted to have the blessing of a wife. Though he was still young, he had always wanted a family. His job never really seemed to be the problem; it was more the women in his life and their lack of commitment. So, for the last two years, he'd left women alone altogether and sank himself into his work and church. But deep down, he knew what he really was doing. ***Running***.

While in Michigan, after a three-year relationship with a beautiful sista named Ranesha, things took a turn for the worst. Ranesha had a sassy short-cut hairstyle, legs for days, and smooth butterscotch skin. Her only complaint was that she didn't get enough attention. So, after working late four days in a row, Evan finally freed up some time. He went to their favorite Chinese food place, picked up some Egg Foo Young, General Tso's chicken, and shrimp fried rice. He even grabbed a bottle of her favorite wine from the local package store. When Evan reached the house, he crept slowly up the stairs to the two-bedroom condo.

He opened the door to find Ranesha sprawled out across their bed, half-naked, clearly being enjoyed as their next-door neighbor Erica's mid-day dessert. She claimed that she didn't know she liked women too, but now it was something that she wanted them to do and experience together. Unlike some men, Evan didn't like to share his woman. Feeling extremely hurt, he packed his things right then and there and drove straight through the night to New York. He was hoping to start fresh.

Unfortunately, New York wasn't any better. Meeting a short, long haired, reserved Latina teacher with grey eyes named Marisa, Evan thought things were going to work out. After dating for eight months, they decided to move in together, and everything seemed to be going great. Until the day he stumbled upon a secret stash of DVDs all starring Marisa. She was using various positions of the Kama Sutra with several men. Sometimes more than one at a time, and none of them was Evan. When confronted, she told him in no uncertain terms that she had a large sexual appetite that he alone could not satisfy. She said that he could either deal with it and love her for who she was, or he could leave. Evan was on a plane to Atlanta that same night.

For Evan, a life with a great career and someone to share it with seemed simple enough. Since he already had a great career that allowed him to travel whenever he needed and paid more than enough, the only thing left to find was the love he could share it with. However, all he seemed to get was love that was either very selfish or love that was way too giving. Not that anything is wrong with giving of yourself, except if you are giving to more than one person at a time and neither was him. Hopefully, a move to the south would bring the peace of mind and heart he longed for.

☀

Vernice was done. No more trying to change the way she thought or how she looked just to accommodate a would-be Mr. Perfect. At this point in her life, she had grown to love herself for who she was. And the Mr. Perfect that was meant for her would have to do that too. If he didn't exist, then that's exactly who she would be with. Herself.

Huh? Who was she kidding? She wanted love just as much as she always had. But this time, if a man wanted her love, he would have to prove it.

Finishing his Frappuccino and muffin, Evan started across the street, back to work when he saw her, Vernice, the girl who worked in photography, down the hall from his desk. Evan had, on very many occasions, dreamed about this voluptuous beauty whom he could easily see come and go from the angle that his desk sat. Vernice had a beautiful caramel complexion kissed by the sun with dark brown hair that seemed to have natural highlights. Guessing her to be about 5 foot 8 inches, she was just the right height with or without heels. But most of all, it was her eyes and her thighs.

Vernice had huge slanted deep penetrating brown eyes with lashes that seemed to sweep her cheeks. She was thick in the thighs, and everything rounded out real nice in the back. A brick house had nothing on her. "Vernice, good morning. How have you been?" Smiling shyly and rushing into the building, she answered, "I'm ok, but I'm kind of running late, so take care." "I was just...." Evan was abruptly cut off by the door closing in his face. He didn't get to say much and kicked himself for not using the time he had better.

Once he was at his desk, Evan got back to work, or at least he tried to. Time after time, he saw Vernice and her thighs sashay by, and he would lose his train of thought. This was becoming an everyday thing, at least for the past few weeks. Apparently, she had just gotten a promotion, so her office was a lot closer. Nodding hello to her, Evan again turned his attention to his writing because this story had to be done in the next two hours. Luckily for him, Vernice would be out of the building doing a shoot for the rest of the afternoon. So, he was able to regain his composure and finish his story on time. Logging out for the day, Evan made sure to leave a copy of his report on his supervisor's desk, then went to the garage to get his car and drive home.

Getting into his black Trailblazer, Evan could think of nothing but a certain Vernice and how early he could get back to work in the morning to see her again. "Ahh, man, I can't be going through this again," he thought to himself. He hardly knew her, but it was just something about that smile and those curves that turned him on to his core. He couldn't understand how this woman with who he barely held a conversation could be such an impact on him. Evan made a promise to himself that he would talk her into having lunch with him before the week was over because all he knew about her now was that every night, she was the star of his dreams.

Chapter 3

After another long week, Vernice announced, "Final shot, ladies. Beautiful. Thank you, thank you, thank you. You guys were great." "Not really," Latonya snickered behind her cup of coffee. "Be nice, Latonya!" "You're my assistant who's supposed to be helping, not starting fights with the models," Vernice shot back. "Well," Latonya replied, "I'm just saying. They kind of sucked. And if it weren't for you, they would look like a bunch of chimpanzees falling all over each other." "Latonya!"

"Sorry, I mean a bunch of beautiful chimpanzees." Laughing, Vernice nodded, "O.k. that's better. Now I'm going home to get a good night's rest. And I suggest you do the same because we have an early shoot tomorrow. This time we're going to have to make a bunch of pigeons look like swans." "Ahh girl, you're crazy." Latonya laughed so hard she started coughing. Vernice looked at her and couldn't help but be touched by her infectious laughter.

Meeting her assistant for the first time a few years ago had been pleasant because she was a person who was looking to learn and grow. Latonya seemed to be grounded, not thinking she knew it all, which was refreshing. Having been a photographer for years now, Vernice often ran into assistants who thought they knew everything. Some who even thought they could take her job. Those assistants usually didn't last long. Saying their goodbyes Vernice and Latonya went home for the night.

Making it home was fairly easy. Five o'clock traffic wasn't bumper-to-bumper, so the usual thirty-minute ride only took fifteen minutes. Now in the comfort of her two-floor townhome Vernice lay across her bed, waiting for the bathwater to fill up. This time of the day was her favorite. The sun was going down and leaving behind traces of reds, oranges, and yellows across the horizon. With the tub now filled with lathery bubbles, she submerged herself into the soft scents of lilac and violets, letting all of the day's worries float away.

Never did she imagine that she would be where she was today. Within the last month, she had actually gotten two promotions and was now making enough money to buy a house and pay off her car in less than a year. She was also planning to treat herself, her mother and grandmother, to that trip to Hawaii they've dreamed of for the last three years. "Thank you, Father," was all she could say because she knew that she had been truly blessed.

Drying herself, Vernice heard her cell phone going off. Grabbing a large towel from the linen closet, she covered herself up and fished it out of her purse, which everyone else called her suitcase. "Hello." "Hey V, it's me, Latonya." "Tonya, do you know how late it is? What's wrong?" Trying not to cry, Latonya explained that she had a family emergency and had to leave town ASAP. "I am so sorry. Is there anything

I can do to help?" "No thanks, but I will be gone for about four weeks. Are you going to be o.k. with all of the shoots that are lined up?" "Of course, the company has temps and seasonal people lined up for stuff like this, so don't worry. You go take care of your family; I'll be fine." "Thanks, Vernice, I'll call you once I have more info and get settled in."

"O.k. sweetie, take care." "You too." Disconnecting that call, Vernice made another to her contact in the human resources department. She needed a temp for her 8 a.m. shoot, so there was no time to waste.

Vernice had been an assistant for years and is now the lead photographer and Creative Content Coordinator at COWIRE magazine. She had worked hard and knew that with all of the competition out there, she had to continue to hustle and provide the readers with the best articles that she could turn out. COWIRE Magazine was cutting edge, focused on the culture's newest styles and trends, uplifting the African American community. It spotlights those creating amazing pieces of Art & Literature, up-and-coming scientists, mathematicians, and architects. If you were the best, you were featured in Cowrie Magazine.

Working hard was nothing new to Vernice but working hard without an assistant was almost impossible. Oh well, things would work out. They had to. And even if she couldn't get an assistant for tomorrow, Vernice would hunker down and make it work until they found someone qualified enough to help her out. The way the light would hit tomorrow, this shoot could not be canceled or postponed. She could hear the sweet voice of her NaNa, who would always tell her, "Never put off 'til tomorrow what can be done today." And Vernice could attribute her success to that very saying.

Growing up poor in the south seemed to be the cliché, but Vernice knew that would not be her story. Having a good bit of street smarts and a great head on her shoulders, Vernice pushed herself to do the best in everything she could. Debate team, Spelling Bee, President of the Beta Club, and Grand Baking Champion of the Home Economics Team. In college, she became Vice President of Student Relations and the Student Body Vice President 2 years in a row.

Vernice did well in everything except sports, but not for lack of trying. Activities with a ball, bat, stick, net, or helmet was not for her. Luckily, she was taught how to swim at a young age, but even that was for fun. She needed to learn to not drown whenever one of her uncles decided to throw or push her into the lake down from her NaNa's house. Now the tables had definitely turned. Whenever there was a family reunion or BBQ at NaNa's house, it was those same uncles that had to watch out.

Five o'clock a.m. was too early for the phone to be ringing. Who could possibly be calling? Trying not to sound groggy, "Hello." "Good morning, may I speak with Ms. Adams?" came a husky voice on the other end of the phone. With caution in her voice, "May I ask who's speaking?" "This is Human Resources down at COWIRE Magazine. My name is

Paul." "Good morning, Paul. This is Ms. Adams. How may I help you?" "Well, Ms. Adams, I see here that you have an application to work for us as a temp." Mariah had forgotten that she and a classmate had gone downtown during the summer and fall months putting in application after application. "Ms. Adams?" Calling her name brought her attention back to the conversation a hand. "Yes, I am still here, Paul." "Alright. I called this morning to see if you would be interested in filling in as a temp today. You seem to have more than enough experience with your college studies. We can start you off with fifteen dollars an hour and see how it goes from there."

"O.k. sure, what time do I need to be in?" "Well, I know it's short notice, but can you be in by 7:30 a.m.? One of our lead photographers has a shoot at 8:00 a.m. sharp, and her assistant is out of town." "7:30 a.m. is fine. Who do I report to?" Mariah yawned. "Report to Vernice Parker and fill out all of your paperwork. "She's probably going to need you all week long, so you will get a whole week's pay. If she needs you longer, she should let you know by Wednesday."

"I will be there, thank you." "Thank you, Ms. Adams. Good luck to you, and you have a wonderful day," Paul stated in a very chipper voice. With that, Mariah hung up and jumped into the shower. She didn't live far from the office building, so Mariah was ready and walking in the door with her coffee cup in hand less than thirty minutes later.

Chapter 4

Vernice looked at her watch for the third time in two minutes. 7:15 a.m. and counting but still no assistant. Pacing the floor, she impatiently waited. The day was not starting out well. First, her neighbors two little dogs were there who playfully attacked her ankles and made her spill her coffee all over her jacket. Then once her clothes were changed, a passing bus splashed water from the streets on her pants.

Thank goodness she always kept an extra outfit at work. Now that she was ready to go, her new assistant had yet to show up. Walking over to her intercom Vernice, paged the front desk clerk. "Yes, Ms. Parker?" "Benita, has the temp arrived yet?" "Yes, Ms. Parker, I just sent her up to your office. Her name is Mariah Adams. She should be there in a minute," Mrs. Benita answered back. Benita Johnston had been at COWIRE Magazine for at least ten years. She was an older woman half Irish and African American. And even though everyone knew she was older because of her mannerisms; nobody knew how old she really was. With her smooth caramel skin, stylish dirty red hair, and big brown eyes, Mrs. Johnston, was all but flawless.

Hearing a light tap at the door, Vernice assumed it was her temp but found it kind of bittersweet that it wasn't. Standing there in his midnight blue suit, fresh haircut, and wing-tipped shoes, was Evan. "Wow!" Clearing her throat, "I mean hello,

Evan. Is there something I can help you with?" Evan couldn't help but blush. "Actually, you can. I know you've been really busy lately, especially since you got your new promotions. By the way, congratulations." "Thank you." "You're welcome, but what I was trying to say is, will you have dinner with me Saturday night? I would really like to get to know you better."

Now just a little lightheaded from the rush of her heartbeat, Vernice wasn't sure what to say. "Evan, I'm not sure. I really don't like to go out with people I work with. The last time I did that, it didn't work out so well for me." Remembering that he promised himself he would not walkway until she said yes, he took a deep breath and tried again. "Vernice, I understand that things might not have worked out for you in the past. But I'm not those men, and I promise that if you don't have a good time on Saturday, I will leave you alone, and you won't have to be bothered with me again. But I have wanted to ask you out for the past three months."

"You have the most beautiful smile, and every time you walk by my desk, I lose my train of thought. So baby, please just put me out of my misery and let me show you how you should be treated." Silence. All Vernice could do was stare into the eyes of this gorgeous man. *No, he wasn't, asking her out.* Usually, she was the third wheel or a backup whenever one of her friend's boyfriends was bringing a friend. How could she trust him? Not only was he 6 foot 2 inches tall, deep brown-grey eyes 275 pounds, and her favorite flavor, dark chocolate; He was also one of the best literary writers in the company and quite the poet. And you know what mama always says, *"If the deal's too sweet, it'll probably rot your teeth."* And this man here was bound to give her a cavity.

"Vernice, please say something." The sound of his voice brought her back to reality. In a whisper, she answered, "Yes, I would love to have dinner with you." "Forget mama," she thought, "I'll just have to go to the dentist." "What time should I be ready?" "Is 7 o'clock o.k.?" "7 o'clock is fine." Evan exhaled, now the huge weight was off of his chest. Slowly moving towards her, he grabbed Vernice's hand and placed a small kiss on the back. Not waiting for a response, he turned and walked back to this desk wondering why in the world this woman affects him so much.

His ex-girlfriend or ex-fiancée never made him feel this twisted and nervous inside. And now that they had plans for Saturday, he was sure his dreams would become more elaborate and give him great ideas on what he could do for her on a later date. Saturday night's date will lead to many more; he will make sure of it. With Evan now back at his desk, Vernice rechecked her watch, still no assistant. Grabbing all of her things, Vernice headed toward her office door. She had to leave now or risk being late.

Ready to go, she opened her door and up walked Mariah, who was trying to catch her breath. "Hi, my name is …" "Let me guess, Mariah," extending her hand. Graciously accepting the handshake, Mariah smiled. "I hope I'm not too late. Paul told me 7:30 a.m., but I figured I would need to get here a little earlier." "Well, I do appreciate that. I don't know why HR would have told you 7:30 a.m. when the shoot is at 8:00 a.m., but let's go ahead and get there. I'll have you scheduled for the rest of the week by the end of the day. By the way, what size shoe do you wear?" "Nine," Mariah stated, confused. "Good, we wear the same size. I have a pair of flats in the car, and I just bought them. You can borrow them till the end of the day." Still confused, Mariah looked down at her feet. "Is there something wrong with my shoes?"

Taking a deep breath and making a mental note to call down to HR for a little one on one when she got a chance, Vernice explained, "I'm guessing you weren't told that our shoot today is on Stone Mountain." Finally catching on, Mariah felt a little embarrassed. "I'm sorry, I didn't know." Waving the apology away, "Don't worry about it; you can put on the flats in my trunk when we get to the site." Pushing the garage button on the elevator, they were on their way.

"Look, I know you know something. I've been coming down here for the past week and a half, my fiancée, is missing. Why won't anyone help me?" By now, Freddie was banging his fist on the officer's desk sitting in front of him.

"Mr. Miles, we have already told you that Ms. Adams is fine. One of the other officers checked out your claim, and she says she is *not* your fiancée. So please do you and me a favor and move on, man!" huffed the rather irritated Officer Cox. Not ready to give up yet, Freddie tried to calm his voice. "O.k., o.k., o.k... Well can you at least tell me where she is so I can see for myself. I just need to hear it from her." Now standing with both hands on his hips. "No! And if I read the records correctly, you like to put your hands on the ladies. Not only am I not going to give you any information, but I'm gonna give you a warning. If you ever come in here again, I'm gonna lock you up in one of those little cells in the basement for harassment. And we just happen to have a lot of very unfriendly fellows down there who don't like punks like you. Now goodbye, Mr. Miles!"

Steaming mad, he stormed out of the downtown Police precinct. If they weren't going to help him find her, he would take it into his own hands. Thinking back, he'd given her everything. He was there for her when she would have otherwise had to drop out of college. Yes, he had to smack her around a couple of times, but that was not his fault. She should have known her position. How dare she think she could just walk out on him? Nobody played with Freddie, especially not with his heart.

"Mariah will pay," he thought to himself. "One way or the other…she will pay."

Spending the week with Vernice had been great, but now it was coming to an end. Mariah hoped that she would be called back to work with her because of all of the fun they had together until Latoya came back. She had never had so much fun working before. On the first day, she changed her shoes, but she still fell on the mountain. Unfortunately, she and Vernice didn't wear the same size clothes, so she was stuck with her fitted skirt. So, while rushing back and forth for different lenses and cameras for the pictures, her new navy-blue skirt hindered one of her steps, and down she went onto a huge rock. Luckily it wasn't a bad fall, so she didn't get any scratches, scars, or bruises. However, her skirt wasn't so lucky, now there were two splits in it. One on each side. And after everyone laughed for about a minute, the rest of the day went great.

Mariah didn't know that photography could be so much fun. She put in an application to be a temp just to get some money while school was out for the summer. It seems that idea has panned out after all. After that crazy day at Stone Mountain, they had shoots at Six Flags, downtown Atlanta, and Lake Lanier Islands. On Friday, there were two shoots at the studio of a local turned national playwright who was making great strides in the African American community. During their time together, she had soaked up all the information and knowledge she could get. Vernice was like a treasure chest, full of gems that she could use to further her career.

She knew that she had been talkative and asked a thousand questions, but Vernice didn't seem to mind. She would take a deep breath and, while shooting, give her the answers she needed and details that she had no idea were even a factor in the world of media and fashion. One thing that really stuck out to Mariah was the view Vernice had on beauty and how the smallest thing could make the biggest difference in a photograph. A sunflower draped across the lap, a drop of water going down a cold frosted glass, or the dimple of a little baby could cause a difference in a regular shoot or a fantastic one. This had to be the most excitement Mariah had seen in years. And even though she was worn out and all she wanted to do was soak in a hot tub of bubbles, it was definitely worth it.

Mariah packed up the souvenirs she got during the week and left the office with a huge smile on her face. As she walked down the street to her car, Mariah felt as if she were being watched. Shaking off her paranoia, Mariah continued down the street, but when she reached her car she was suddenly grabbed from behind.

Her screams cried out, but they fell upon no one's ears. It was later than she thought it was, and everyone had already gone home. As Mariah turned to face her attacker, her eyes widened, and panic set in. "Fredrick! How did you…?" was all she could manage to say. He covered her mouth with something, and an undeniable urge to sleep came over her, then everything went dark.

Chapter 5

Tonight, was the night. Evan had been waiting for this date since the first day he saw Vernice. Looking in the mirror at his new suit and the smile on his face, he laughed at himself. How after all he had been through, could he be so smitten over a woman? You would think that he would be bitter. But he wasn't. Evan had been raised by his mother, and as a single mother, she didn't play any games with him when it came to relationships. She raised him to be respectful and a bit of a romantic. So, the mistakes of his past two relationships would not get in the way of him finding true love. They had hurt and, at one point, placed doubts in his mind as to what kind of a man he was. Evan knew that to keep moving forward, he had to keep his faith and remember not only who he was, but Whose he was.

Looking over his clothes again, making sure that everything was perfect, he grabbed his key off the mantel in the living room and headed downstairs. Once he got into his car, Evan uploaded the address Vernice sent to his intern earlier that week. Seconds later, the directions were up, and he was off. Arriving at her apartment no more than 15 minutes later, he took a deep breath, walked up to her door, and knocked.

Hearing a loud knock at the door, Vernice glanced at the clock. He was right on time. She was impressed. "Who is it?"

she called, already knowing exactly who it was. "It's Evan." Hearing his name sent a tingle up her spine. Pushing that aside she walked over to the door.

When she opened it, all she could do was gasp. At work, he looked good, but now he was gorgeous. "Oh, my," managed to slip from her lips. Not able to hold back a slight laugh, Evan was flattered. "Is that a good or bad, "Oh my?" Because I'm hoping that it was good. If not, I'm gonna have to go out tomorrow and buy a new wardrobe and kick the guy's butt who sold me this suit." And there was that smile again. It was not fair the things his smile could do to her. "No, it was a *very good* Oh my. I can't believe I said that." shyly looking away.

"Well, thank you, and might I add that you look extravagant in that blue. I think I now officially have a new favorite color." There it was that smile of his again. How did he know just the right time to show those pearly whites? And *no, he didn't* just lick his lips. Vernice had to find a way to stop thinking to herself and invite him in. "I'm sorry, please come in. I just have to grab my shawl, and we can go." Stepping inside, Evan didn't want to venture too far, so he just stood in the doorway. Watching Vernice walk around had become one of his favorite pastimes, so he was more than happy to stand there and watch her. Making her way down the hall, Evan noticed that she walked into the last door on the right. He wondered if that was her bedroom. Boy, did he want to find out soon, but the gentleman in him wouldn't allow him to go there. Not just yet anyway. So, he stuck his hands in his pockets and tried to think of something else.

"You have a pretty nice apartment here," he yelled. "Thanks" was all he could hear coming from the room. Two minutes later, Vernice had her shawl, and they were on their way. "I hope you like Italian. There's a great restaurant not too far from here that I think you might like." "I love Italian food. Have you been doing some spying on me or something?" "Just a little," showing a small measurement of space in between his fingers. "Guess I'll let you off the hook this time. Besides, it couldn't have been too hard to figure out that I love pasta and bread with all of these hips." "Hey, I just so happen to like those hips." "Mmm-hmm," flipping her hair, Vernice couldn't help but blush. This guy was starting to give her butterfly guts.

"Are you always so…?" "So honest?" Evan said, trying to finish her sentence. "No, actually, I was going to say charming." "I don't know about being charming but, my mom did raise me to believe a woman should always be treated with the utmost respect. And when you find one that's special, you should treat her right by showing her just how special she is." "Your mother was kind of a romantic, huh?" "Yes, she was, and I guess a lot of it rubbed off on me." Realizing that the car seemed to have warmed a little, Vernice let the shawl drop off her shoulders, and they both sat in silence for the rest of the ride. Not because they didn't have anything to say, it was because they couldn't deny that there was a serious attraction going on between them. But neither knew what to do next. So, they just enjoyed the rest of their night together, holding small talk about the job and some childhood adventures over the food and wine.

Vernice had chicken and spinach manicotti, while Evan enjoyed the house lasagna. Dessert came in the form of a dark chocolate raspberry cheesecake that they tried their best to split down the middle. The ride home was tense, filled with an unspoken desire that both Vernice and Evan couldn't deny. They could only pretend to be interested in the city life around them, watching the hustle and bustle of the nightlife in the ATL with all the lights and neon signs. Losing control now would only complicate things and probably end the relationship before it could get started. As a gentleman, Evan walked Vernice to her door, kissed her on the cheek, and rushed home to a very much-needed ice-cold shower.

Chapter 6

"Ms. Adams, Ms. Adams, can you hear me?" Slowly regaining consciousness, Mariah opened her eyes to the sound of her name. Everything was foggy, and she couldn't quite focus her eyes enough. "Ms. Adams, if you can hear me, my name is Doctor Peterson. You are in the hospital, but you're going to be fine." "Hospital?" Mariah echoed. "Hospital, why?" "Ms. Adams, you were assaulted, and one of your co-workers saw a man trying to put you into a car, and well, I guess he scared him off and called the police. "Right now, I just want you to get some rest, but later on, there are a few detectives who would like to ask you some questions."

Detective, that's it. Mariah remembered the detective who warned her a few days ago about being careful. Between her blurred vision and the huge headache, she had, she wished she had listened. "Doctor, please wait," she groaned. I need to speak to Detective Robins. I know he can help me. Please I need Detective Robins." "O.k. I'll tell the officers in the waiting area and see what they can do. In the meantime, just rest. There's an officer at the door, so that you won't be bothered." And with that, he left her to sleep.

Knowing there were police watching outside her room was definitely reassuring, but who was this co-worker that the doctor was talking about? She hardly knew anyone in the company. All of her time there was spent with Vernice, and last she checked, Vernice was on her way home to get ready for her hot date. As fatigue took over, Mariah knew she owed this mystery co-worker a lot. But for now, her body demanded sleep, so she closed her eyes and dozed off.

Waking up to a beautiful sunrise was always Evan's favorite thing, but now he had the urge to wake up to something even more beautiful. A Ms. Vernice Parker. As a reminder, every bit of that urge was bulging from beneath the covers. Pushing that aside, Evan said his morning prayers. He loved to thank God for waking him up every morning and for the strength and wisdom to make the most of every day. Morning prayer was something that used to get him laughed at all throughout college. Now those same guys who dogged him about glorifying God every time they got the chance were the same ones who either never finished college or were now sitting in the pews with him every Sunday morning.

After another cold shower, Evan dressed and started preparing breakfast. He was usually the one who cooked in his relationships. Just another good trait his mother instilled in him. He made waffles, eggs, sausage, and a small cup of fruit medley. As he sat down to eat, there was a light tap at the door. Who could it be at 7:30 a.m. knocking on his door? Then it dawned on him, it was Saturday, and the neighborhood kids would go around and dump everyone's garbage for a few dollars. "Hold on," he said as he gathered up his trash bags.

He opened the door and slugged the two large garbage bags out without even looking. "Here you go." "Evan!" "Vernice, I am so sorry. I thought you were the little kids who get the trash."

"Obviously," she giggled as she looked down at the two black bags that struck her in the legs and now lay on top of her shoes. "I am sorry." Embarrassed, Evan quickly removed the bags and invited Vernice in.

"Please have a seat. Are your legs o.k.?" "Yeah, they'll be fine. I brought your jacket back. You let me wear it last night, and I figured you would want it back," she stated, knowing that was not her true intention for showing up. Vernice handed Evan his jacket then sat back down. Looking around, she was impressed. "You know, I don't know too many brothers who are single and without kids that have a home like this, "gesturing to the spaciousness and calmness of the area. He walked back in from the closet, where he hung his jacket. "Well, Ms. Parker, contrary to most stereotypes, there are a few of us brothers who like to own property and have a plan before we start a family. We don't need a bachelor's pad, so to speak, to make us feel manly." "I wished more men thought like you. I've only been getting to know you for not even 24 hours, and your ideals and morals continue to amaze me."

Trying not to blush, Evan changed the subject. "As much as I would love to continue this conversation, I am starving. Since you're here, would you like to join me for breakfast?"

"Oh, no, I wouldn't want to intrude." "Please, I have plenty." Escorting Vernice to the dining room, Evan fixed her a plate. "Wow, this is delicious. Thank you," she told him. Evan nodded his head. "So, let me get this straight, you're a gentleman, a property owner, great at your job, and you cook! You're just one surprise after another, aren't you?" Looking into her eyes and saying with all the heat he now felt inside, "Well, just you wait the shows just beginning." Before she could respond to his seductive suggestion, Evan leaned over and gently placed a kiss on her lips.

Vernice didn't know what to do, so she did the only thing she could, and that was give in to him. She wrapped her arms around his neck to draw him in closer. The warmth of his juicy lips was hypnotizing. As Evan's hands dropped down her back, headed towards what he had wanted to hold all morning, Vernice's phone went off loudly. "I'd better get that," she stated. Pulling himself away from her with all the strength he could muster, he whispered, "I know, but who is calling you this early on a Saturday anyway?" Placing her hands on his chest to calm herself and to place some space in between them, "I'm not sure, but the sooner you remove your hands, the sooner I can find out." "O.k., but hurry back. I still have to show you the deck out back."

Running into the living room, Vernice grabbed her purse and answered the phone. "Hello, yes, may I speak to Ms. Parker?" asked the voice on the other end. "Yes, you may," Vernice countered. "This is she. May I ask what this is about." "My name is Doctor Peterson, and I have a young lady by the name of Mariah Adams under my care. She has you listed as her employer."

"Wait a minute," Vernice interrupted. She's in the hospital; what happened?" "I can't give you all the details Ms. Parker; they are confidential. And I really just called to verify her employment. Does she work for you?" "Actually, she's been my assistant this week. My regular assistant had to go out of town." "So, you've only been her employer for one week?" "Yes, I was hoping to keep her on for a little while longer. Is she o.k.? Is there anything I can do? How long is it going to be before she can return to work?" "Ms. Parker she is going to need about two to three days. If you would like, I can get some papers drawn up for you. I should have them ready by this evening. I can fax them to you, or you can pick them up if you were planning on coming down here to visit." "I'll be there as soon as possible." "Alright, I will see you then, goodbye." "Goodbye Doctor."

Chapter 7

Hiding away was something Fredrick did best, and since his last little charade, he knew he needed to lay low. "She thinks she can avoid me," he said to himself. "Well, not if I have anything to do with it." He'd found her once again, and if it wasn't for some hero wanna-be he would have her right where he wanted. Now he was gonna have to come up with yet another plan on how he could get her, and after all this trouble, she was gonna get it.

They are guarding her room, so he needed to tread lightly. Luckily, he had a contact down at the hospital, who informed him about when she was getting discharged. From the records that had been faxed over, Mariah was now conscious but still very weak. So that gave him at least a few more days to perfect his next ploy, and this time no one was going to stop them from being together. Not even her.

Hanging up the phone, Vernice filled Evan in on what was going on. I have to go see how she's doing. Will you come with me?" "Of course, I will," Evan said with no hesitation. "But you seem kinda shaken-up," he told her. Picking up his car keys, "So I think we should take my car." "O.k., I guess. But I'm not shaken up, just a little worried. Doctor Peterson said that it was Paul who brought Mariah to the hospital." "Paul? You mean the guy from Human Resources?" "Yeah, isn't that somethin? He's the one who called her up for me. Evan, if it wasn't for him staying late last night, who knows how bad things would have gotten." "Well, we don't have to worry about that now. Mariah is going to be fine, so relax." "I'll be able to relax when I see her. I mean, who would do such a thing?" Standing outside on the porch, Evan locked his door and hurried to catch up with Vernice. "Shall we?" He offered his arm, and Vernice graciously accepted it.

Arriving at the hospital, Evan let Vernice out at the door so that he could park the car. By the time he met her inside, Vernice already had gotten the floor and room number. Walking down the hallway, they could tell exactly which room belonged to Mariah, especially with the two officers seated in front of the door. They approached, and Vernice said softly, "Hello. We are here to visit Ms. Mariah Adams." One of the officers stood up abruptly, then pulled out his notebook and pen. "Names?" "Oh, I'm Vernice Parker." Gesturing toward him, "This is Evan James." "Wait here." "O.k."

Seeing her nervousness, the other officer stated, "Don't take it personally. We've been working together for a year now, and he always talks in two or three-word sentences." "Oh o.k. thanks, that was kinda weird." The door opened, and that same non-verbal officer stood holding the door and said, "You're cleared." They both looked at his partner for understanding. "That means you may enter." "Thanks,"

Evan whispered to that officer as he escorted Vernice past the police guard.

Mariah smiled as soon as she saw Vernice. "Hey, y'all!" "Hi, yourself," Vernice smiled back. How are you?" "Much better now that I have regular company. The only people I've seen have been doctors and cops. Please come on in, have a seat and make yourselves at home or at least a little comfortable." Did the cops find out who did this? I mean, cause you look a hot…."

"Evan!" Vernice interrupted. "I was just asking about what happened." "It's o.k., you two. I already know who did this and it's my ex-boyfriend. I have been running away from him for the last few months, but he found me again. The doctors said he used something called chloroform to knock me out. If it hadn't been for some mysterious co-worker, I would probably be in a lot more trouble." "So, you mean you don't know who caught him?" Evan asked.

"No, I don't, but I wish I did. I owe that person a lot, and if you don't mind, as soon as I get out of here, I would really like to stop by and do a little research to find out who it was." Waving her comment away, "Girl, please, you rest up. I'm on it. I'll have a name for you by Monday, noon." A sadness arose on Mariah's face. "Vernice, thank you so much. I hope this doesn't ruin my chances of working with you. I know you didn't have to come down here, but this means a lot to me."

Vernice placed her hand over Mariah's. "I have had a great time working with you too, and if you would like, I would love to have you come back and work with me once you're o.k." "Besides, everybody has things in their past that may cause problems in the present. But the key is not only to move on, but to learn from those mistakes and not make the same ones over and over again."

Leaving the hospital, Evan and Vernice were exhausted. As much as he wanted to spend the rest of the day with her, he didn't want her to feel smothered. So, after putting Vernice into her car, he trailed her home. Walking her to the door, Evan placed a kiss on her forehead and started to leave, only to be surprised by Vernice grabbing his hand. Turning to look at her, he saw in her eyes exactly what she wanted.

Vernice gazed into Evan's eyes as she moved closer to him. "Would you like to come in?" "Are you sure?" he asked. He had to know where her heart was. With a soft whisper, "Yes," left her lips. "But if…?" He tried to counter. "Shh." She covered his lips with her finger. Speaking softly, he moved her hand. "Vernice, as much as I want this now, I can't. I made a vow that the next time I made love to a woman, it would be on our honeymoon and that neither of us would leave our room for at least three days."

"So please don't take this the wrong way, but unless you want to go down to the courthouse right now, I need to leave. And please stop looking at me like that before I lose my mind." "You know, you never cease to amaze me, Mr. James."

"Hey, like I told you before, this is just the beginning." "The beginning? Huh? Wait a minute, Evan. Are you trying to court me?" "Ms. Parker," he asked, "Would that be such a bad thing?" Silence.

Trying to hide the grin that was spreading across his face he said, "Then I guess this is goodnight." Finally speaking Vernice told him, "I guess. Will you come by in the morning for brunch?" Bowing as a gentleman, "It would be my honor." "O.k. Evan, see you about 11:30 - 12:00?" "Will do." Stepping inside, Vernice turned back slowly. "Bye, sweetheart," was all he said and was gone.

Closing the door, she relived his last words. "Bye, sweetheart," kind of made her feel like a schoolgirl all over again. Were there still men who treated women with such care, or was this how he got to all his women? At this point, Vernice didn't know, but he sent tingles up her spine and a few other places, for that matter. But for right now, she was content with where they were and could not wait to see where things would go.

On his way home, Evan couldn't help but fantasize about Vernice. Had she not meant so much to him, he might not have been able to hold on to the morals he had and stick to his guns. But he was glad he did. After the drama he has been through, he knew he couldn't afford to mess up now. Things seemed to be going so well with Vernice, and already she had shown him that there was more to her than he thought. When they first met, her innocence was such a turn-on. But after today, her not- so-much innocence, had turned him on even more.

As Evan pulled into his driveway and planned to try to re-focus his energy on work, his cellphone rang. "Hello?" "Hey man, it's Paul. Are you busy?" "No not really but, I've had a long day already. Whatz up?" "Well, I wanted to talk to you about something, but in person, not over the phone. Evan, is there someplace we could meet later?" "You sound like this is serious. Is everything alright, man?" "No, not really." Letting out a long sigh, Paul told him, "There's some mess that went down, and I'm not sure what to do."

"Tell you what; give me thirty minutes I'll meet you down at Big Tony's pizzeria." "Thanks, man, see you then." "No problem, Paul. See you later." Evan ran inside to change clothes, use the bathroom, and then headed out.

Chapter 8

After ordering a pitcher of beer, Italian sausage, and pineapples on a large pizza with extra sauce and a twenty piece of honey buffalo wings, Paul sat back waiting for Evan to arrive. He had to tell somebody and knew that if anybody understood him or at least knew what he should do, it would be Evan. Since day one, Paul and Evan clicked. They started at COWIRE within the same week, and even though they both worked in different positions, their paths often crossed. It didn't take long for them to realize they liked a lot of the same things. Neither Evan nor Paul really had any family in town, so he and Paul became quick best friends.

As the waitress placed the cold pitcher of beer on the table, Evan walked into the crowded pizzeria, and it wasn't hard to find Paul. He was seated in their usual spot. They would meet at Tony's on a regular basis, at least once a week, to shoot the breeze, but today was different. Something was wrong, and it was written all over Paul's face. "Hey man, whatz up?" Evan started reaching his hand out and gave Paul some dap.

Taking one more gulp from his mug, Paul cleared this throat and began, "Man, you won't believe what I got into this weekend. It started Friday at work. A few new hires turned their information in late, so of course, I was told to stay late and update the system. That was the good part of my night. When I was leaving, minding my own business, I saw that new temp that I called in this week walking to her car. Now when I first talked to her, I thought she sounded kind of cute, and even when she showed up for work, I gave her about a seven, maybe eight. That night, though, baby girl was looking fine. So, you know me, I'm gonna try to see whatz up. Right before I could, some high yellow punk grabbed her from behind and was trying to put her into her trunk." "What?!" "Yeah, man, so I ran up on him and put him in the chokehold."

"You put him in a chokehold?" Evan asked. "Yeah, man, I don't know what got into me. I just ran up on him. Then he tried to put that same rag he had over Mariah on my face. I tripped him up and put him in a headlock. The next thing I knew that punk went to sleep, so I let him go."

"What? Man, why you do that?" Evan was stunned. He couldn't believe that the guy who saved Mariah was his boy Paul. Who would have thought? "Yeah, man, I let him go and ole yellow hit the floor." Paul flopped back down in his seat because talking about the incident had gotten him all excited as if he were reliving it. "I was so crunk, man, that I almost forgot about baby girl." "So, it was you who saved her that night," Evan whispered as not to draw any further attention to their conversation. "I don't know about all of that man. After ole dude was out, I just took Mariah to the emergency room. The doctors are the ones who saved her." "No man, please," waving his hand in the air, "You saved her cause you're the one who stopped her crazy ex-boyfriend from kidnapping her. Matter of fact, the police were looking for you after you left the hospital."

"Police, man, I don't know bout all that." "Come on, man, they want to thank you, not lock you up." "Still, I don't know about talking to the police." "Well, you're gonna have to," Evan told him. "The nurses already told them that whoever brought her in was a guy who worked with her. They have a sketched picture of you and everything." "Man, you lying!

"Yea, I am," Evan said, laughing. "But only about the picture. They are looking for you." "So, what am I supposed to do, turn myself in or something?" "You're a hero, Paul. They just want to know who you are and to verify who the guy was." "A hero, huh?" Sitting back against the booth, "I kind of like the sound of that." "Well, you aren't superman." "No, I'm not, but I did save the damsel in distress, didn't I?"

Now feeling proud of himself, Paul took a big gulp of his beer and dug into the now steaming hot pizza that lay between them. "Whatever, man." Watching Paul gloat about being a so-called hero, Evan wondered how he would react if he ever saw Vernice being attacked. Would he be able to disarm her attacker and save her? Paul took him by his arm and shook Evan out of his daydream. "Huh?" "Man, what are you thinking about?" "Nothing." "Yea, right. So, what you think? Imma get an award of something?" "I don't know about all that, but you might get the girl!" Almost choking on his pizza, "What do you mean get the girl?"

"Exactly what I said. Mariah wants to know who it was that helped her out. And if you play your cards right, hey, who knows. I'm telling you now, though, if you tell her I said so, I'll call you a liar to your face." Rubbing his hands together, Paul let out a sneaky laugh. "Hmm… that's whatz up. I appreciate the 411 man!" Interrupting his thoughts, "Like I said, I will call you a liar. Beside Mariah's a nice girl, so if you're gonna go after her, your gonna have to play it cool." Paul apparently got distracted by the football game on TV, so Evan leaned and hit him on the arm. "Huh?" "Man, did you hear me?"

"Yeah, yeah, yeah, she's a good girl, so be nice. I got you, man. Besides, I've seen her around the office, and honestly, she doesn't seem like those chicken heads I usually mess with, and I don't want her thinking I'm some ruff neck. Evan, man, I'm kinda feelin baby girl." "I hope so cause by jumping into her business on Friday; you could have gotten your butt whooped." "What? Man, please, ole boy never had a chance." Laughing, Paul and Evan sat back and enjoyed the rest of their pizza while watching the game.

Now recovered from her assault, Mariah packed her things to go home. She could think of only her night and shining armor. Who was he? What had made him intervene for her that night? How did he look? Mariah felt a sense of intrigue and obligation. She felt she owed him so much. Throughout her life, she'd been around many men who treated her wrong. Her mom always called her a bum magnet, and this last relationship was the worst. She couldn't believe it had come to this, but it had.

She had actually been hospitalized for four days, and Lord only knew how she was going to tell her mother. Throughout the whole ordeal with Fredrick, she tried to give her mother the least amount of information as possible. Now, after this, no more secrets could be held. At least that much was clear. Unfortunately, the truth would be coming out a lot than she thought.

Leaving the closet, Mariah turned and was shocked to see there standing in the door was Mrs. Adam's with her arms folded. The look on her face was mixed between disappointment, hurt, and disbelief. Mariah told the nurse earlier that she didn't have anyone to pick her up from the hospital, so she would be taking the bus home. Apparently, that didn't fly because against her wishes, the nurse contacted her mother, and there she stood.

"You have some explaining to do, young lady." "I know, mom. I'm just really tired right now." "That's fine, but you *will* fill me in later once you've regained your strength. Mariah, I didn't rush down here to argue and fuss. I just came to take my secretive daughter home. But we are going to have that talk. Comprende?" "Comprende." "Good, now give me that bag, and let's get out of here."

Chapter 9

Back at home, Vernice sat on her patio, sipping her coffee. She had a crazy weekend. There had been more excitement this weekend than had happened to her in the last ten years of her life. She hoped Mariah would be o.k. Mostly her mind stayed fixed on Mr. Evan. Things between them seemed almost electric. Vernice hoped Evan felt the same way, and according to his reactions, he did. Looking off into the distance, Vernice laughed at herself. She couldn't believe she had almost slept with him, but even more so, he turned her down. Not because he didn't want to but because he really cares about her. As she remembered how he spoke to her and wanted to make love to her, Vernice started having tingling sensations from the top of her spine to the core of her thighs. Shaking herself out of her lustful thoughts, Vernice got up and went back inside to get ready for her day. Putting the finishing touches on her make-up, Vernice heard a knock at the door. Filled with anticipation, she ran out of the bathroom.

Opening the door, Vernice became breathless. The shock on her face made the delivery boy laugh. "Are you Ms. Vernice Adams?" asked a very tall and lanky young man. "Yes, I am." "Well, these are for you." The young man handed Vernice a huge vase holding 24 yellow, orange, red and pink carnations. "Oh my, these are beautiful." Vernice's heart began to swell. Where had this man been her whole life?

Had she met him years ago, she would have been spared a lot of heartache and pain. Then again, if she hadn't dated some of the jerks that she did, she might not have realized what a good man Evan was. "Well, ma'am," the delivery boy said, "I'm glad you think so cause… fellas!"

Stepping to the side, he made room for the three other delivery boys to walk up to Vernice with three more vases of flowers. The second vase held 24 lilies, and the third vase held 24 sunflowers, and the fourth had 24 orchids. Once all delivery boys were tipped and gone, Vernice turned to view all of her flowers. She couldn't believe someone would do all of this for her. Flowers were everywhere, and the room now smelled like a tropical forest.

"Woo…" softly escaped her lips. Everything that this man did was above and beyond what she expected. Vernice opened the card that was seated inside her carnations, and it read, To: My precious flower, your smile makes my day bloom, so I hope these flowers make your day as happy as you make me. Evan. XOXO.

Vernice was completely speechless. This kind of stuff only happened in fairy tales. Who knew there were still real gentlemen in the world? She had only gone out with this man once, but they had seen each other every day since then.

Evan was turning out to be everything that she never knew she wanted in a man. He had been through some bad relationships, that is apparent, but it doesn't seem to have changed him. Or maybe it had. But definitely for the better. Picking one of her carnations, Vernice pinned it to her pink suit jacket and left for work.

Freddie was seated across the street at the cafe, looking around outside of COWIRE Magazine. He watched everyone who went in and out of the building, hoping to see a glimpse of Mariah or at least see that nosey wanna-be who foiled his plans of getting her back. "Who did he think he was anyway?" he thought to himself. "Didn't he realize who he was messing with?" "Excuse me, sir," said the waitress. "Is there anything else I can get for you today?" Freddie snapped at her, "Did I call you?! Now shoo! You're bugging me!" As he turned his attention back to the COWIRE building, he saw Paul walking up to the front door.

"Gotcha!" he smirked to himself. He then got up from the table where he had been holding up for the last three hours, paid for his drink, and dropped fifty cents on the table as a tip. Leaving the diner, he pulled his hoodie over his head to not be recognized. Making his way across the street, he ran up close, trying to blend in with the crowd.

As Paul went about his usual routine and approached the elevator in the back hallway, Freddie saw his shot. Keeping enough distance, he waited for the elevator doors to open. No one was around, and this was his chance. As the elevator doors opened, Freddie ran up and pushed Paul hard into the elevator, and he fell right into the arms of two U.S. marshals.

"Oh snap!" Freddie turned on his heels and bolted towards the front door. Paul spun around as soon as the marshals helped him catch his balance and immediately recognized his assailant. "That's him!" The marshals grabbed Paul, putting him in between them for protection. They drew their weapons, but the elevator doors had shut on them by the time they tried to run after Freddie. Paul and the marshals went over what had just happened on the way back up to his office desk.

Marshal's Webb and Terri had come to talk with Paul about the assault on Mariah. Apparently, this wasn't Freddie's first attempt at kidnapping her or having a run-in with law enforcement. "You were very lucky, Mr. Rayne's. Had we not been in that elevator, there's no telling what he would have done. Freddie is very sneaky and not totally sane, especially when it comes to Mariah. We know you were instrumental in helping her escape his grasps last time, but now it seems he's coming after you." "Yeah, I saw. I can't believe he had the nerve to come and try to yank me on my job. Now I know he has a few screws loose."

"Not that many. He had sense enough to wait until you were alone. Or so he thought," Marshal Terri added. "One good thing out of all of this is that now we have a more current picture of him. Your cameras were able to catch a picture of him walking up to the building before he put that hoodie over his head. Now, if you want, we can have a patrol car follow you because if he found you and singled you out here, then he's probably been watching you."

"Who's been watching you?" They all turned to see Evan standing there. "Excuse me. This is a private conversation. Please come back to see Mr. Rayne's later," directed Marshal Webb. "Oh, he's o.k," Paul told them. "This is my friend and co-worker Evan. He already knows about the whole thing." "Is everything alright, Paul? Who's been watching you?" Sucking his teeth, Paul answered, "That punk Freddie who tried to kidnap Mariah." "Well, how do you know he's been watching you?" With a defiant attitude, Marshal Terri interrupted, "We know because he just followed Paul inside the building, and if it weren't for us, he would have probably tried to kill him." "Hold on, hold on," jumping to his own defense, "He might have gotten the jump on me, but there wouldn't have been no killing goin on."

"We don't have time for a debate, Mr. Raynes. We're going to put an unmarked car upfront and down in the parking deck until you get off. Then Marshal Webb or I will be at your house across the street. If he strikes again, we'll have him. We are going to let you guys get back to work, and Mr. Raynes, we'll be seeing you around." After the marshals left, Paul told Evan everything that happened, and they both decided it would be a good day to go home early. They made plans to meet up later at Evans' house for Monday night football and brews.

In her office, Vernice replayed the whole weekend in her mind. She hadn't had this much excitement since she went to

Germany to visit her pen pal Gebhard. In the last year of high school, she decided it was time to lose her virginity, a decision she would take back if she could. At the time, the thought of going across the world to another country was exciting. What she didn't expect was to get back home and realize that not only had he taken her virginity, but he had given her an S.T.D... Vernice's memories stopped abruptly when there was a tap at her door.

Sticking his head inside, Evan whispered, "Hope I'm not interrupting you." "Of course not, come on in," Vernice told him. "I was actually just thinking about something." "Oh really?" "Yes, really. But on a lighter note, what did you think about this weekend? Kind of wild, huh?" "Wild is not the word," he told her. "This weekend was… a hot mess." Laughing, "That pretty much sums it up. "

"Well, if you think that was something, Vernice, you're going to love what happened today." "Today? What did I miss?" "Do you remember Paul Raynes? He works in human resources." "Yeah, he's the one who hooked me up with Mariah. Why? What happened to him?" "You have to promise me that you won't tell anyone." "Tell anyone what, Evan?"

"Well, first, you're gonna have to promise me you won't tell anyone *and* seal it with a kiss." "A kiss?!" "Yes, a kiss." "I don't know about all of that. What if someone walks in on us? I can't be seen making out in my office." "Making out?! Girl, where is your mind? I said a kiss, a little peck." Crossing his arms. "Sooo, you wanna make out, huh?" picking at her slip of the tongue. "No, that's not what I meant." "Well, what did you mean, Ms. Vernice? You said making out." Stepping closer, he asked, "Do I need to lock the door?" "Evan, no, look....mmmmwaa!" She planted a wet one right on his lips. "I'll take that as a yes, and I know you can do better than that," he smirked. "But it will work for now." "Now you're not being fair, Evan." "Hey, I never said that I was fair. As a matter of fact, what I told you was that you wouldn't regret going out with me." His cockiness made a little wet spot in Vernice's favorite navy-blue panties. "True," barely escaped her lips. "And you did enjoy our weekend together, didn't you?" "Yes." "Well," he said, "Then give me another kiss."

And before she could object any further, his lips were on her mouth, drawing every breath out of her. Then he slowly backed away while he watched her come back down to earth. "That is so not fair, Evan." "There's that word again. Besides, like I said, there's nothing fair in love and war." Crossing her arms, "Who said anything about love?" Evan laughed, "Sweetheart, right now we are at war and believe me when the battle is over, you will be in love."

Never before had a man shown so much interest or made her feel so wanted. Vernice couldn't help but question her feelings. Was he serious, or was he playing games? Did he really want to be with her? Make love to her? Maybe he was just putting on a show to make her lower her guard so that he could have his way. She decided she had to know because, at this point, there was an undeniable attraction between them, and curiosity was seriously killing her cat.

"Evan, I'm going to be honest with you. I did enjoy our weekend, and I am attracted to you, but I want you to answer me honestly. Why me? What is it about me that you like? There are so many other women, not saying that I'm not fine cause I am, but what is it about me that made you decide to ask me out? I'm not about games." The fact that she asked why, made Evan take a step back. "Yes, sweetheart, you are fine," closing the gap in between them again. "And please listen carefully to what I'm about to say next. From the first day I started working here, you and only you have been the woman who caught my eye. I don't know if it was your beaming personality, those hips, or the way you smile."

"Maybe it's the way you lick your lips before you start a presentation. I'll admit I was a bit scared to ask you out at first, but now that I've got you in my grasps, I don't plan on letting you go. Now I was going to tell you what happened this morning, but you've got me all hot and bothered. So, before I lay you across your desk, I'm going to go cool down somewhere and just call you later to let you know what happened."

Jumping in front of him Vernice blocked his way. "Hold on, I gave you your kiss, so you have to tell me... something!" "In a nutshell, Paul is the one who helped Mariah, and her crazy a** ex-boyfriend just tried to jump him up in the elevator. But he got ran off by two big country-looking marshals." "Oh my!" Vernice gasped. "Oh yeah." "Well, what are they going to do?" "I'll tell you later." Closing the door behind him, Vernice yelled, "You better."

Chapter 10

More restless than she ever thought she'd be, Mariah sat in the kitchen listening to her mother rant and rave about how wrong she was. "Mother, please, stop yelling. But mom...Mom. Yes. Yes, ma'am." All she could get out for the first twenty minutes of their conversation was, "Yes, mother." Finally, her mother calmed down and simply stated, "You really hurt me, Mariah. You could have been killed, and I wouldn't even have known who to go after with my shotgun."

Mariah giggled, "Ma, I am sorry, I didn't want you to worry about me. You have enough drama on your plate as it is. Besides, I thought he wouldn't be able to find me anymore. I guess I was wrong!" "Well, I guess so. You are my daughter, my baby. Forget everybody else and anything else. *You* are the most important thing in this world to me. I will worry, because I have the right to worry about you. Don't you dare try to take that from me. You hear me, girl?"

"Yes, Mama, I am so sorry. I promise I'll keep you in the loop from now on. I just wanted to protect you. I never meant to hurt you. I just know how you are. And yes, you may be good with your shotgun, but Fredrick is crazy ma. It's bad enough that he's after me, but to have him trying to get to you as well. I couldn't deal with that." "I tell you what,

Mariah, one of my old Soros has a timeshare not far from here. How about we…?" "Nope!" "What do you mean no? I didn't even finish my statement," her mom squealed. "I know, but I'm not running anymore. I am so tired of running." Mariah's eyes filled with tears, and her emotion came through clearly over the phone. "My life will never be the same again if I keep running and being scared. I mean, look at all that's happened so far. It's time to stand up for myself. I've been in constant contact with the police department, and as soon as Frederick rears his ugly head again, they're going to make sure he goes down."

"Wow, Mariah, I don't think I've ever heard you sound so determined before. I am almost speechless." both women fell out in laughter. Now with raised spirits, Mariah told her mother how much she loved her and promised to call her back later. After hanging up with her mom, Mariah called Vernice with no luck. "Hello, you've reached Vernice. Sorry I missed you." Mariah hung up and was about to take a nap when her cell phone went off.

It was a text message from Vernice, and it read, "Good morning sunshine hope you don't have plans today. I just talked to Evan, and now I know who your knight in shining armor is. Be at my place by six. We have a lot to talk about, girl. Txt me back if u can't come ASAP." "Yes!" Mariah said out loud, and with no hesitation, she ran into her bedroom. She threw on her fitted Baby Phat jeans, her favorite carnation-colored tank top, and some flip flops her mom bought her from Wal-Mart. Even though the shoes only cost

$1.00, they were one of the most comfortable pairs she had. Pulling her hair up into a ponytail, Mariah spread some lip gloss on her lips, grabbed her keys, and ran out of the door heading straight for COWIRE magazine.

"Ms. Vernice, you have an unexpected visitor," said Ms. Morris over the intercom. "Yes, Ms. Morris, who is it?" "Ms. Mariah is here to see you." "Well, of course, let her in." Before Mariah could reach the door, it swung open. The ladies embraced each other like two sisters who hadn't seen each other in years. "How are you, girl?" "Better, a lot better now," Mariah told her. "Good. Now not that I'm not delighted to see you here, but I thought that I text you about dinner?" Picking up her cell phone, Vernice checked to make sure the text went to the right place. "Yes, you did text me about dinner, but you also told me you knew who saved my life."

"Dinner can wait, but that piece of info, a sista like me needs now." "Well, someone is mighty anxious now, aren't we." "Whatever!" "It's cool, I'll tell you." Leaning over her desk, Vernice placed her head in her hands. "I want you to think back. Do you remember the husky-voiced brother who called you from human resources to come in and work for me?" "Yeah, a Paul something or another. I remember that name and that voice. Does he know who was there late that night?" "Well, It just so happens that a little bug on the wall told me that *he* was the one who stayed late that night."

"What?!" excitement filled her voice. You mean the sexy-sounding brotha who called me into work here is the same one who kept that jerk from kidnapping me?" "That's exactly what I'm saying." "I don't believe this! I have to talk to him." Gathering her purse, "Where does he work? What floor?" "Well, hold on Mariah, pump your breaks. There's more." "More? What's more?" Settling back in her chair, Vernice explained.

"Apparently, Freddie knew who Paul was before I did. He attacked him this morning on his way into the building." Slowly Mariah's expression went from excitement to horror. "Oh no. Is he o.k.? What happened?" "He's fine, calm down." It was too late. Tears were already dropping from Mariah's eyes. Vernice handed her a tissue, "Calm down, girl. He ran off when he saw the marshals who were here to interview Paul." Mariah questioned, "Marshals!?"

"From what I was told, Freddie was going to try to hurt him, but the two marshals who came to talk to him were actually in the elevator, so he bolted. Paul is fine; he went home early to rest. He and Evan are supposed to meet up later for a football game." "Oh really?!" Mariah asked with a sneaky smile across her face. "Oh no!" "OH YES, Vernice." Even though she hadn't known Mariah that long, she knew that sneaky look anywhere, and it could only mean trouble. "No, Mariah. What are you thinking about?" "I'm thinking that I like football."

Chapter 11

Mariah and Vernice stood in the mirror, putting the final touches on their outfits. "You look, fabulous darling." "I know, Mariah, but I still think this a bad idea. Evan and I have really clicked, and I don't want to mess it up by just popping up on him. You know how men are with their football, and it's the Jaguars game tonight. I just don't know, girl." "Vernice, he might not like us popping up on him at first, but I'm sure he'll be more than happy once he sees the way your girls are popping out of that top you have on."

Mariah had picked out the outfit for Vernice to where. A black low-cut V-neck blouse paired with dark, fitted stretch jeans, strapped sandals, and a soft blue silk scarf. The perfect weapon to divert Evan's mind away from the fact that they were intruding on his boy's night in. "Hey, you can't talk. Your girls aren't hiding either. And Mariah, your skirt may be long, but girl, it would be taking your pulse if it got any tighter." Laughing, "I know. I do look sexy, don't I? Do you think I should put something shorter on?" "Mariah!" "Hey, I'm just saying. If Paul looks as good as he sounds, you may be riding home by yourself tonight!"

Pulling her hair behind her ears and putting on her diamond studs, Vernice shook her head. Mariah may seem to be a good girl at first, but the more she got to know her,

Mariah was kind of a freak, but undercover with it. You wouldn't know unless she wanted you to. Guess birds of a feather do flock together.

Oblivious to the fact that they were being watched, Vernice and Mariah continued to play around in the mirror. Finishing up, they grabbed their purses and started to leave. Mariah exited Vernice's' apartment first. Just as Vernice was about to lock the door, she went back in because she realized she'd forgotten her little bottle of mace and her shawl. Grabbing them quickly, she threw the mace into her purse and placed the shawl over her arms. Stepping back out into the hallway, Vernice locked the door and turned around only to see the horror-filled eyes of Mariah.

To the side of her head was a 9mm gun, and holding it was a lazy-eyed slender male with light eyes and light skin. So, it had to be… "Freddie!" "Yes, Ms. Parker, I see you've heard about me." Panic started to set in, but Vernice knew better than to let it show; it would only feed into his craziness.

Mariah whispered, "Vernice, I am so sorry about this." "It's not your fault; you have nothing to apologize about." "Oh yes, she does. Baby girl has been hiding out trying to get away from me, and that's just not nice now, is it Mariah?" Freddie squeezed tighter on the hold he had around her waist.

"Now we are gonna go have a talk, and since you know who I am, you're going to join us," pointing the gun now at

Vernice. "Now move!" Letting his grasps on Mariah go, Freddie followed the two of them outside and guided them to a car he had waiting nearby.

"Yeah, yeah, in yo face," Evan screamed, "That defense ain't no joke playa." "Whateva man, you might as well go on and calm down. You know how my boys like to come back." "Come back? Boy, please! You had to have *been there*, before you can come back." "Oh, that's cold." "Yes, but true." Evan lifted his can in a toast. Paul mumbled under his breath, "You better toast yourself."

After the game, Paul paid up. "$20, $40, $60, $80, $100.00 dollars. I got to stop betting you." "I've told you that before, especially when it comes to my Jags. But until you learn, I will be more than happy to take all your money." "As a matter of fact, I'm going to use this to surprise Vernice with a romantic night out on the town."

Rubbing his chin, Paul asked, "Speaking of, how's Mariah been?" "She's doing good, from what I hear. Matter of fact, I heard she came up to the job today to see V." "For real?" "Yes, they've gotten pretty cool since they started working together." "So, you think they might wanna come ova and hang out." "You know what, Paul? That's the best idea you've had all day. Hand me my phone over there. Dialing the phone, "I'll call her right now."

"Shut up back there! Ain't nothing wrong with you." Vernice had stuck her phone in her bra before Freddie took her purse, and fortunately, it was on vibrate. Leaning forward, she quickly tapped the screen, hoping it would answer. Evan called out on the other side of the phone, "Hello? Vernice?" Hoping it would give a hint, she said out loud, "Look, Freddie, this isn't going to help anything!" "Shut up!" he told her. "Where are you taking us?" Turning in his seat, Freddie pointed his gun in Vernice's face and screamed, "I said shut up before I… just shut up!" Mariah knew this rage and quickly jumped in, saying, "She's sorry, Freddie, she doesn't understand. Remember your beef is with me, not her."

Slowly calming down, he turned his attention back to the road. "Your best bet is to keep her quiet. We'll be home soon, and I wasn't planning on company, but I'm sure you'll both be comfortable." Both women looked at each other and mouthed the word, "Home?" It was now clear how crazy Fredrick was. His reality is so screwed that he thinks he is simply taking Mariah home.

Looking at the shock on Evan's face made Paul nervous "Man, what's wrong?" "Shh..." "What she say?" "Shh, Shh." Paul got up from his seat and walked over to stand in front of him. All of a sudden, Evan jumped up and grabbed Paul by the front of his shirt, saying, "We got to go. Now!"

"What the He**, man?!" "It's Freddie." "Freddie?! You mean, Mariah's Freddie?" "Yes, he's got her and Vernice."

"Man, we gotta do something." "Wait a minute, Paul, are those marshals still following you?" "Yeah, I think so." "Good, then they should have followed you here. Let's go." Grabbing their keys, Evan and Paul ran out the door.

Sitting across the street sat an unmarked car. Paul recognized it as the one that had been following him all day. The lights came on and blinked twice, then went back off. Walking up to the car, Paul yelled, "Look, forget about Freddie trying to get me. My boy just got off a crazy phone call, and he could hear that Freddie's got Mariah." "What?" Marshal Terri grabbed his walkie-talkie. "Bradshaw, check in," he shouted.

"Who's agent Bradshaw?" Evan asked. "Bradshaw is supposed to be following Mariah." Back on his walkie-talkie, "Webb, you there?" A groggy voice answered back. "Terri, somebody hit us, and I think Bradshaw's gone." "D***! Don't worry; help is on the way. Just hold on, man, hold on." Looking up at Evan, "This is very important. What exactly did you hear?" Now standing beside him, he explained everything he heard.

"If I'm not mistaken before the phone went dead, I heard Vernice whisper about the old cotton mills." "I know that area, they turned those buildings into lofts." "Yeah, well, they were in that area when the phone call cut off." Having enough information to start tracking them, Marshal Terri turned on the car's engine. "O.k. we've wasted enough time. You two go in the house and lock the doors."

"No way, man, we're helping. If it wasn't for us, you wouldn't have even known what was going on." "Young man, I know you want to help, but you are interfering with a federal investigation." "Well, arrest us then, cause if you're not, we are helping!" "That's right," Evan chimed in. They both stared Marshal Terri down as if there was nothing he could say or do to change their minds at this point.

"Fine, give me your phone. I'll have Vernice's cell number tracked, but I'm telling you now, when we find Freddie, you stay back. Stay in your car because if I have to shoot you to get to this psycho, I will. Do you understand me?" "Understood." Evan tossed his phone to Marshal Terri, and then he and Paul ran to the car and waited for him to pull off. If they both weren't worried enough, the rain definitely didn't help. This weather would make tracking her phone harder to do and calling Vernice back, and at this point, it is just too risky.

Chapter 12

Ten minutes had passed since she had answered her phone, and she hoped to God that Evan was still there. "Welcome home baby girl." Frankie smiled like a kid on Christmas day. "I have missed you sooo.... much, Mariah." Fredrick put the car in park, then opened the door for Mariah and Vernice. "Now, ladies, I have put my little friend away, but if you start being silly, I will pull him back out, ok?" Both shook their heads. "Good. Now, shall we?" Holding Mariah's hand tightly as if they were in love. Freddie escorted them around a set of apartments down an alley and into the backyard of an old broken-down house where he had apparently set up residence.

"Freddie, what's this?" "This is our new house, sweet thang! Now I know before you told me that you were tired of living in an apartment. You wanted a house that you could call your own. And maybe before, I wasn't determined enough, you know. Since you've been gone, I realized that it wasn't you. It was me. So…" Freddie scooped Mariah up in his arms, kicked the door in, and carried her across the threshold. Vernice knew that if she was going to bolt, this was definitely the time; still, if she did, she would be leaving Mariah alone to deal with a man who was unmistakably in love with her; but, also unmistakably out of his mind, and that was a bad combination.

Fredrick must have sensed her hesitation because he quickly put Mariah back down onto her feet and grabbed his 9mm out of his pants. "Don't even think about it, Ms. Lady. Get on in here." Just as quick as the chance was there, it was gone. "Come on in here with your feisty self." Looking over at Mariah. "She keeps that up; I might just have to keep her around." He fixed his eyes on Vernice and winked.

Suddenly Vernice felt a cold chill shoot down her spine. There was no way she was going to be a part of his sick little fantasies. "Now, you two play nice. I'm gonna go start on dinner. "Mariah, It's your favorite tonight, baby. T-bone steak, twice-baked potatoes, and broccoli spears. Y'all go on and have a seat right here on this nice plush couch, and I'll be back in a minute." As soon as Frankie was out of sight, they began to plot.

"Vernice, I am so sorry I got you into this." "Don't you dare. This isn't your fault. But hey, at least I get a great meal before I…." "Don't even talk like that!" Mariah interrupted. "I'm just playing, honey. The Lord wouldn't have brought you or me as far as he has for it to end in this place."

Looking around, Vernice noticed a stench in the air that couldn't have been dinner unless Freddie was even crazier than she thought. "What is that smell?" "I don't know," Mariah said, "But it's making me nauseous. It almost smells like…." Her heart skipped a beat, and she lost her whole train of thought when she noticed a pair of shoes half burnt in the fireplace. "Oh no," she gasped. "What girl? What's wrong with you? Mariah, you're scaring me." Crying and becoming frantic, she covered her face as she pointed to the fireplace and asked, "What is that?"

By now, Vernice realized what Mariah was looking at, and all that she could think was that crazy, sick, lunatic. "Look at me, Mariah." "But…what *is* that? *Who…* is that?" "I think that's what we've been smelling, sweetie. I don't think that Freddie got this house legally."

On the road now, Evan sped past the other cars on the street. He ran red lights and didn't stop for anyone. He was doing a great job of tailing Marshal Terri. They knew now where Mariah's phone had stopped moving. It was just a matter of reaching them before anyone got hurt. Neither Paul nor Evan had much to say at this point. Evan was too busy concentrating on his driving and praying that nothing had happened to Vernice. He cared about her so much more than she knew. Paul was also in another world during the drive.

For most of his life, he was the one on the other side of the law. Lucky that gave him an edge; he knew how to hide out from the po-po. This skill set would definitely come in handy tonight. "Paul and Evan, come in," Marshal Terri called over the walkie-talkie he'd given them before pulling off. "We're here, and we are about to come up on the tracked location, so slow it down." "10/4." Both cars slowed.

They stopped about a block away from the location where the cell phone signal was lost. Getting out of his car, Marshal

Terri waived Evan and Paul over. "Now look, I know you two had some ideas about how this was going to go down but make no mistakes, kids play is over." Sighing, "I called for back-up, it is on the way, but everybody was tied up and won't make it for at least 10 minutes." Pulling out his gun and cocking it. "Unfortunately, that punk in there killed one of my men. So, forget back-up!"

He handed the 9mm standard issue to Evan. "Do you know how to use this?" "Yes, sir." Marshal Terri then pulled another gun out of his ankle holster. What about you, Paul…?" Before he could finish his statement, Paul had already withdrawn his own 22 from the back of his pants. "Yes, she is registered," he said looking at his gun. "And I never leave home without her." "That's all I need to know," Marshal Terri told him. "Now from the readings on this G.P.S., they're not in the lofts, but somewhere around them."

"I know this area pretty well. There are some abandoned houses around here, but most are occupied, and the residents would never let a nut like Freddie anywhere near their house." Thinking harder, Paul remembered, "But there are a few older homes owned by the elders in the community. They refused to sell when the newer homes were being built. He could be in one of those." "Good idea. How many of those are within a block?" "Maybe three, but one of those got condemned because a few of the street pharmacists around here used to use it as a crack house after the owner died. No matter how crazy he is, he's not in that one." "So, where's the other two? "Follow me," Paul told them, leading the way.

They came upon a small two-bedroom house with boarded-up windows and a young woman sitting on the porch braiding her daughter's hair. "O.k. let me handle this, you two. Stay back until I see what's going on." Almost immediately, Marshal Terri returned. "Well," Paul asked, "What happened? Is he hiding in there?" "No, but when I asked about the girls, she said she saw a dark-skinned and a light-skinned girl go into Mr. Carton's house across the alley. She didn't pay any attention to it cause they were dressed like hookers."

"Hookers? Naw, that couldn't have been them," Evan quickly interjected. "Hold your horse's big boy, don't be so defensive. Often, the perp will make his woman dress the way he wants her to in situations like this. He may be playing out his sick fantasy on both women."

"In any case, we need to check it out. Let's go. And remember to keep your heads down. I don't want to shoot one of you two knuckleheads, but if I have to, I will. In my book, you don't kill a cop and get away with it."

Chapter 13

"Alright, ladies, dinner is served." Freddie entered the room and brought two trays with him. Vernice's eyes slid closed because she was surprised that the food smelled delicious. "Ah huh," Frankie snickered. "Looks good, doesn't it?" Quickly changing her expression, she threw her head back, "It's alright, I guess." Laughing now, he told her, "You know what? I'm liking you more and more." Turning his attention to Mariah, "Baby girl, are you o.k.? You haven't been talking much."

"What do you want me to say, Fredrick? I've tried to tell you over and over again that what we had is over. I'm not your baby girl anymore." He waved her comment off as if she hadn't said a word. "You're just upset with me for interrupting your girl's night out. But you shouldn't say things like that, especially after I've made this beautiful dinner for everyone."

Now becoming upset and shaking his finger at her, "You think you're slick you… you… you… (stuttering). You're not going to ruin this night with that nonsense. So be a good girl and eat your dinner. I have white chocolate chip brownies in the oven and coffee ice cream for dessert." "I don't want your food, Fredrick."

"It's Freddie! Stop calling me Fredrick! You know that drives me crazy." Suddenly, the phone rang three times then stopped. "You know what? I'm gonna see whose calling and eat my dinner in the kitchen so I don't burn the brownies that we have for dessert." Walking off, Freddie started mumbling to himself.

Setting down the serving tray Freddie already knew who was calling. Picking up his house phone, he hit number two on autodial and waited for an answer. "Aye, Freddie, what are you doing, man?" "Cuz you kinda caught me at a bad time" "A bad time? Look, I stuck my neck out for you last week giving you that information on your girl. I thought you just wanted to talk to her and get closer"

"Yeah, that's all I wanted at first, but when I saw her..." "But nothing, man, you used me. I get in to work today, and here there is an APB on her and a coworker." "Ah, I don't know what you're talking about." Freddie tried to laugh it off. "You are a whole lie because they have a BOLO out on you. I know one thing; I know they better not find out I had anything to do with your mess. Do you know what happens when a cop goes to jail?"

"Shut up, sounding like a punk. Nobody is going to find out anything cause there ain't nothing to find out. Even if there was, how stupid are you to be calling my house from the precinct. If you needed to call me, I told you to go down the street to that café that don't have no cameras and call me from there." "Forget you, man! I better not go down for helping you." "Shut up and get off my phone. I have company, and you are blowing my mood. And don't call me back with your crooked self. I don't know If I can trust you anymore, but you should know that if anything goes wrong and I feel like you double crossed me, I'm coming for you. I know where you *and* your mama stay.

Mariah began to panic. "You know pissing him off might not be the best thing to do right now." "Well, I had to do something to get him out of here," Vernice told her. "Why?" "Well, there's a little opening over there in the curtain, and girl, God is good." A huge smile settled on Mariah's face. "Yes, He is. But what are you smiling about." "Remember that guy Paul you were telling me about?" "Yeah, what about him?" "Is he kinda light brown, tall, and not skinny but thin built?" "Yeah, why?" Not being able to hold in her excitement, "Cause I just saw him with Evan and some big ole mechanic-looking guy!"

Freddie yelled from the kitchen, "Quiet down in there, you two." "Sorry, babe, just joking around." Vernice shot Mariah a look with a raised eyebrow. "Hey, gotta keep him in there somehow. Plus, if he thinks he's getting to me, he might let his guard down some more." Vernice winked, "Gotcha." "Hope you guys are almost ready in there. The brownies will be out in a minute." "Sounds great!"

Vernice noticed their untouched plates. "Mariah" "Huh?" She turned her attention back to the situation at hand. "What are we going to do if he comes in here and sees we haven't eaten your favorite meal. He's gonna flip." "First of all, this is not my favorite meal. It's Freddie's favorite meal to cook for me because he likes to put an x-pill in the steaks and the potatoes." "You gotta be kidding me." "No, not really. I only realized it the last time he cooked it because I caught him right before he was bringing it to me." "Did you eat it?"

"That's a story for another time. Right now, give me your plate. I know exactly what to do with this. While I dispose of the food, you need to look over there." Standing at the window was Evan. She smiled, and he waived. "What are you doing here?" she slowly mouthed so he could read her lips. "You'll see in a minute." Evan placed his finger over this mouth to signal Vernice to be quiet.

Re-entering the room, Freddie brought dessert, and not a moment too soon; Mariah had just set their plates back down with nothing left but the potato skins, forks, and knives. "Well, I see you two enjoyed your meals. How you feeling?" "To be honest, I feel pretty good, Freddie, really good!"

"Great, how about you, my chocolate drop?" He tightened the scarf hanging around Vernice's' neck even though nothing was really wrong with it. She could tell by the sneaky grin on his face that Mariah was right. He had doused the food with drugs. So, it was probably in her best interest to play along. "Actually, I think that was the best steak I've ever had." "I was hoping you would like it," Freddie replied.

Unbeknownst to Freddie, since he'd been conversing, the three men had let themselves in through the back door in the kitchen. "Shh, we cannot let him know we're in the house, do you understand?" "Yes," Evan and Paul said in unison. "Good, now stay here. I'm going to go around to those stairs."

"Maybe I can see better over there. I suggest you get ready. With this nut job you never know." "You know what, Marshal Terri? That couldn't be truer."

"I see you brought company," Freddie demanded in a loud, deep voice, pistol in hand. "Now get up!" "How did you know?" "Cause I'm Freddie baby, and because I put a silent alarm on the doors. It went off in my ear the moment you came in. I must admit I didn't think you'd find me."

Realizing who had come with Marshal Terri, "Oh, and you? What are you doing? What did you think you were gonna do? You have a whole lot of nerve, man, but that's o.k. I think Mr. Carton has some room left for you. O.k., all three of you get in the living room, Now!!!" As they entered the living room, it was now apparent why the girls hadn't given them a heads up. Freddie had them tied together back-to-back on chairs in the middle of the room. "Get on in there and join the party, boys."

Seeing Vernice tied up with tears in her eyes gave Evan a huge lump in his throat. He had to do something and now. Right then, red, and blue lights flashed inside the house. Marshal Terri knew what that meant. Back up had finally arrived. Evan must have read his mind because they both turned on their heels and attacked.

Evan grabbed the gun while Marshal Terri and Paul tackled Freddie to the floor. All the lights went out throughout the house, as the doors were broken down. Within seconds it was over. Or was it?

Freddie was handcuffed and picked up off the floor.

As the ropes dropped from Vernice, she stood looking for Evan and saw that he was down. Her heart skipped a beat. This time it wasn't from the warmth of his touch. It was a cold chill from the thought that she would no longer be able to feel his chest against her cheeks or his lips upon her hand. Marshal Terri, along with two paramedics, lifted Evan to his feet. What she had dreaded was true; Evan had been shot. Vernice replayed everything in her head. The gun went off twice; Evan was only hit once, in the arm. Thank God he had only lost consciousness due to the shock of being hit. So, where was the other bullet?

"Vernice," a soft voice called behind her. As she turned, Mariah collapsed into her arms. The bullet had ricochet and hit Mariah in her stomach. "Help! Somebody, help me!" Vernice cried. Paul appeared at her side and scooped Mariah out of her arms. They ran her to one of the ambulances waiting outside and rode with her back to the hospital.

This was not how Mariah saw this ending. Here again, she lay in a hospital bed because of Freddie's craziness. The good news is that it was an in-and-out bullet wound, so no vital organs were hit. And now there is so much evidence stacked against Freddie.

Luckily, she would be released later that week. What seemed to be a lifelong nightmare for Mariah was now over. Walking out of the courtroom hand in hand, she and Paul smiled at each other. Her wound was still sore, and even though she was still healing, she had a man by her side that was determined not to let her lift a finger until she was completely well. Plus, with all of the painkillers she was on, Mariah couldn't feel anything anyway.

The best part of all was that Freddie wouldn't see the light of day with her testimony for at least 20 years; starting with an additional two years in an asylum for rehabilitation. Now she was free to live her life without looking behind. She got a best friend out of the deal and a new boss. Vernice and Evan were able to pull some strings without involving Paul to get her a full-time position as an additional photography assistant in Vernice's department at COWIRE Magazine.

As far as Evan and Vernice were concerned, they were definitely in love and showing each other how much as often as they could. A beautiful ring sat perfectly on her *right* ring finger. They agreed that it would be at least a year before any real plans were made. Life took on a whole new meaning for them because they both began seeing life with a whole new perspective.

Sometimes life is hard and scary, but if you hold on through the drama and stress, life can be blessed, beautiful, and filled with love.

The End

SOMETIMES LIFE!

www.ingramcontent.com/pod-product-compliance
Lightning Source LLC
LaVergne TN
LVHW020655100826
845148LV00012B/2499
* 9 7 8 0 5 7 8 3 5 3 2 8 9 *